The Lighthouse Cat

By Sue Stainton
Illustrated by Anne Mortimer

KATHERINE TEGEN BOOKS
An Imprint of HarperCollinsPublishers

To Mark,
and a special thank-you
to Mum and Dad

—S.S.

To Sue

—A.M.

Acknowledgments
With thanks to Trinity House, Plymouth City Museum, and the
Association of Lighthouse Keepers for all their help with the research
for this book; and many thanks to Plymouth City Council and every-
one involved with the renovation of Smeaton's Tower, for allowing us
to explore the lighthouse, climb the scaffolding, and touch the weather
vane while the lighthouse was strictly under wraps.

The Lighthouse Cat
Text copyright © 2004 by Sue Stainton
Illustrations copyright © 2004 by Anne Mortimer
Manufactured in China by South China Printing Company Ltd. All rights reserved.
For information address HarperCollins Children's Books, a division of HarperCollins
Publishers, 10 East 53rd Street, New York, NY 10022.
www.harperchildrens.com

Library of Congress Cataloging-in-Publication Data
Stainton, Sue.
    The lighthouse cat / by Sue Stainton ; illustrated by Anne Mortimer.
        p.   cm.
    Summary: When a fishing boat is caught in a storm, a lighthouse cat named Mackerel
gathers other cats to try to help out.
    ISBN 0-06-009604-7 — ISBN 0-06-009605-5 (lib. bdg.)
    [1. Cats—Fiction. 2. Lighthouses—Fiction. 3. Rescue work—Fiction.]
I. Mortimer, Anne, ill. II. Title.
PZ7.S782555 Li 2003   2002020682
[E]—dc21   CIP
                                                                                        AC

Typography by Al Cetta and Drew Willis
09 10 11 12 13 SCP 10 9 8 7 6 5
❖
First Edition

The Lighthouse Cat

The old lighthouse stood proudly on the very edge of the rocks and sparkled its message over every mood of the sea.

Blue seas lapped and whispered, green seas danced, and every once in a while black seas raged.

The lighthouse was watched over by only a straggle of sugar-cube cottages that balanced high up on the edges of the cliffs, crawling slowly down to a fishing village farther along the bay.

You could scramble down the slippery rocks but the only easy way to the lighthouse was by boat.

At the very top of the old lighthouse, the great twenty-four-candle lantern sent its light nearly as far as the sky.

At dawn, yawning, the lonely lighthouse keeper scanned the wide ocean for ships.

Keeping the candles lit was his most important job.

Without fail, his pocket watch would remind him to check the lantern light and trim the candlewicks every half hour.

It was well known that without the old lighthouse, the jagged rocky coastline would be littered with shipwrecks.

Every Friday, if the sea was friendly, a boat from the fishing village would bring supplies to the lighthouse keeper.

On one particular Friday, he piled the boxes high on the round kitchen table and realized it was already time to check the lantern.

Up, up, up he climbed, to where the twenty-four candles glowed obediently.

Sometimes the lighthouse keeper would try to make things more interesting and gallop up, up, up three steps at a time or hop down, down, down on one leg, but usually he plodded.

Down, down, down he went, thinking of lunch, and suddenly rolled head over heels. *Thump, thump, thump,* all the way down, down, down.

There he found himself nose to nose with something.

The something had bright yellow eyes and was swirled with stormy colors of silver shadowy fish.

When the something meowed, the lighthouse keeper chuckled and called him Mackerel.

Then he laughed and laughed and laughed.

This was the best thing in this week's groceries!

The two became inseparable.

Little Mackerel would follow the lighthouse keeper everywhere.

Up, up, up. Down, down, down.

Mackerel made friends with the seagulls and puffins and explored every nook of the rocky outcrop.

He gazed at himself in the rock pools and quickly learned about crabs and slippery seaweed.

Mackerel knew how to scan the sea, and when he spotted a whale or a boat, he would tap the lighthouse keeper's nose or jump onto his shoulder.

Every night without fail the two of them would go up, up, up to the very top of the lighthouse, watch the night seas, and keep the candles burning.

Sometimes, on sunny days, they would add
another coat of paint to the lighthouse's red and
white stripes or sit on the very edge of the rocks and
watch for dolphins.

When the tide was really low, they would scour
the beach and collect driftwood so that on stormy
days the lighthouse keeper could set to work on his
curved and round furniture.

Once they even found a message in a bottle.

The lighthouse keeper loved his lighthouse, with
its round rooms. Now he whistled and was never
even the tiniest bit lonely.

With Mackerel, the lighthouse was the best and
only place in the world.

And still without fail they would check the
lantern light every half hour.

Every day and every night was the same, except for one.

It was known and feared that in times of terrible storms the candles could blow out.

One dark night the black clouds gathered speed and whisked through the heavens. The sea leaped in a frenzy at the command of the storm, the waves rose ever higher, and the moon kept blinking as it was buffeted by the wind.

In one huff the wind gathered all its strength and blew out the candles in the lighthouse as though they were on a birthday cake.

Now the lighthouse stood blind, as the wind spiraled delightedly around.

Shivering, Mackerel gazed hard out to sea, watching a small fishing boat disappear and reappear through the mountainous seas, ever drifting toward the jagged-toothed rocks. Was that two eyes flashing at him from the boat?

Where was the lighthouse keeper?

For an instant the moon lit up Mackerel's yellow eyes, and he fled down, down, down.

Then, out on the rocky outcrop, Mackerel saw the lighthouse keeper frantically waving a lantern. But the wind blew that out too, like a feather.

Mackerel knew what he had to do. He sped up, up, up to the top of the lighthouse and caterwauled and screamed at the top of his voice to the heavens.

For a moment the wind stopped to listen.

Mackerel's yells reached the twitching ears of every cat sleeping in the cottages dotting the high cliffs.

Then eleven cats, also caterwauling and screaming, came slipping and sliding, running, jumping, and tumbling down the cliffside. In the chaos, plant pots crashed, fishing nets unraveled, and onions and potatoes bumped down the cliffs after them.

Within minutes, eleven wet and wailing cats
had sped up, up, up to the top of the lighthouse.

Mackerel was waiting; one by one each jumped up
next to him and gazed at the thrashing fishing boat.

All twelve cats called to the moon, and again the
wind stopped to listen. The clouds parted, and the
moon peeped through and reflected in the cats' eyes.

At that very moment the lighthouse keeper
looked up in desperation.

He saw twenty-four little lights at the very top of
the lighthouse, where the lantern should shine.

Surely the fishing boat must see them!

Up, up, up the lighthouse keeper ran.

He watched, wide-eyed.

He hoped.

He prayed.

Then, very slowly, the little fishing boat turned miraculously away from the rocks.

Again, Mackerel saw the two eyes flash back at him from the boat.

The twelve cats all looked around and smiled.

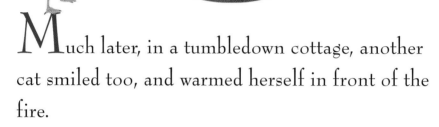

M uch later, in a tumbledown cottage, another cat smiled too, and warmed herself in front of the fire.

The village people never knew about their cats that night.

They still talk about the great storm and how their cats slept for a whole day and night afterward.

What would have happened had the great lighthouse lantern blown out? they wondered.

Little did they know!

THE LIGHTHOUSE

This story is inspired by a lighthouse called Smeaton's Tower. It stood for one hundred twenty-seven years at sea on the treacherous windswept Eddystone rocks just south of Plymouth, in the southwest of England.

There have been five lighthouses on those rocks.

The first, Winstanley's wooden tower (1698), was also the first-ever lighthouse surrounded by deep water, proving that a lighthouse could save countless lives. It was rebuilt after the first winter but was washed out to sea four years later in the most terrible storm that had ever been recorded in England.

The third, Rudyerd's Tower (1709), burned down after forty-seven years, when the twenty-four candles set fire to the roof. Luckily, the three lighthouse keepers were rescued; one had swallowed seven ounces of melted lead as it dripped from the roof!

The fourth, Smeaton's Tower (1759), then still lit by twenty-four candles, inspired lighthouse design around the world. When the rock started to erode, the people wanted the lighthouse brought to land, and it has now stood on Plymouth Hoe for more than a hundred years. This lighthouse appeared as a feat of engineering on the old British penny coin.

The only one of these lighthouses not to have been powered by candles, Douglass Tower (1882), now with its own helipad, still stands on the Eddystone rocks today.

We can only guess how many people these five windswept lampposts of the ocean and their keepers have saved from the wild sea and dark rocks.

There was certainly no lighthouse to guide the Pilgrims, who sailed from Plymouth to America in 1620, past these dangerous reefs.

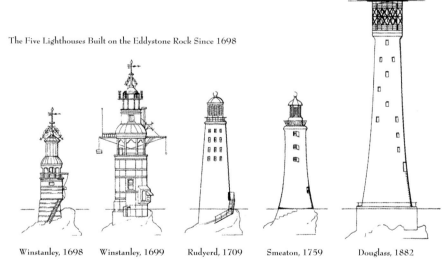

The Five Lighthouses Built on the Eddystone Rock Since 1698

Winstanley, 1698   Winstanley, 1699   Rudyerd, 1709   Smeaton, 1759   Douglass, 1882

Trinity House Collection

SELECTED BIBLIOGRAPHY

Palmer, Mike. *Eddystone 300: The Finger of Light* (Torpoint, Cornwall: Palmridge Publishing, 1998).
Tarrant, Michael. *Cornwall's Lighthouse Heritage* (Truro, Cornwall: Twelveheads Press, 1990).

By Friday, when the sea was all its iridescent shades of blue again, the boat turned up with supplies.

Mackerel felt sure he had seen the boat somewhere else, and when a cat the color of night, with flashing eyes, looked out and smiled, he knew where he had seen those eyes.

Now, every night, whistling twice as loud, the lighthouse keeper still sits with Mackerel and his new friend.

Together they scan the sea and watch the glow of the great lantern creeping far and wide, as the sun sets and the moon rises.